Where we are going to next

Flash Fiction by

Amy Foster Myer

Finishing Line Press
Georgetown, Kentucky

Where we are going to next

ACKNOWLEDGMENTS

Argemina's Revenge: originally published in *SmokeLong Quarterly*, March 2020
Cul-ti-vate: originally published in *Ariel Chart*, Dec. 2018
How We Do Things Around Here: originally published in *Blue Five Notebook*,
Winter 2017

Publisher: Leah Huete de Maines
Editor: Christen Kincaid
Cover Art: Ksenia Chernaya via Canva
Author Photo: Sarah Schultz
Cover Design: Elizabeth Maines McCleavy

Order online: www.finishinglinepress.com
also available on amazon.com

Author inquiries and mail orders:
Finishing Line Press
PO Box 1626
Georgetown, Kentucky 40324
USA

Table of Contents

Argemina's Revenge 1

cul•ti•vate 4

Laqueum quia Claire... 7

How We Do Things Around Here... 10

Check one, check check.. 12

a pair of red curtains 15

Measure twice, cut once... 18

Funeral Pyre 21

Hook, Lift, Release... 24

Cotton Trail Queen 27

We See She.. 30

*This book is for Sarah, my first and best reader,
my eternal desert island companion.*

Argemina's Revenge

My daughter is careening around the backyard, running in circles with her body tilted toward the ground, seeing how far she can angle before she falls. I stand at the window with the cordless, listening to the hospital social worker explain my mother's recent episode. As is inevitable, my daughter falls over and laughs and reaches her arms out, embracing empty air.

Argemina!" she yells. "You nut." It's what I tell her when she's being wackypants.

The social worker is saying my name. She's saying they're adding dissociative disorder to my mother's diagnosis. Fine, I say, sounds good. There's a pause; she knows I've not been paying attention. Her sigh tells me she is a mother too, that she understands there is only so much attention you can give two people at once. They will call me with updates, she says, and my mother will likely be released in another week or two, once the medications have taken over, evened out. As soon as she stops talking to people no one else can see.

At the fish store, my daughter gazes, mouth agape, in front of the wall of tanks. Mollies. Tetras. Guppies. Black-finned sharks, cruising lazily. Bun-bun dangles from one hand, the other extended, hand hanging limp, as though it's wrapped around the shoulders of a child beside her.

"Over here," I call and she drops her arm, ambles over, calling Argemina to follow when she has apparently remained by the cichlids.

"We want two angelfish," I tell the clerk, a high school boy. "A breeding pair."

He nods thoughtfully and bends, hands on knees to examine the tank. "No way to tell which are breeding. No way to tell if they're even boys or girls." He winks at my daughter. He gets a net and a baggie and lifts the lid. "They either mate or one [kills] the other." He mouths it but my daughter is astute.

"Kills?"

"Whoops," he says, "Sorry."

I flap a hand; a problematic word being spoken in front of my daughter ranks pretty far down the current list of concerns.

It is a laborious process, but there are two he's noticed keeping

1

close together most of the time, swimming in tandem. "Best friends," he says.

"Like me and Argemina!" my daughter chimes in, her arm back to hanging mid-air, her hand giving a quick loyal pump as though there's a real shoulder she can feel under her palm.

So slowly I want to gouge my eyes, fish-boy dips the net and trails behind the two he has in mind. The fish within spring to frenzied life, the whole tank taking on the look of an animated Escher sketch. How he keeps track of these two is beyond my abilities; they all look the same to me. But then there they are, in the bag. He explains which type of tank we want, which type of filter, which type of substrate.

"Not rocks," he corrects when my daughter and I both gravitate toward ones that glow under a blacklight. "Sand," he says with authority. "The eggs will fall between rocks, the fry will get lost and can't get back up. With sand, the angel mommy can scoop the eggs, the fry, and keep them safe."

What about the invisible fry-friends, I want to ask, how will she know where *they* are?

He sends us out the door with a good luck and two lollipops clasped in my daughter's hand, neither for me.

My mother and daughter sit at a table and play checkers. It is her favorite thing about when Grammy "goes on vacation." I would buy a set for home, but something about it feels accusatory, as though if we had checkers in our house, it would be like saying it's just a matter of time. Which it is.

A woman shuffles over, heavily-drugged. She reaches for the third chair but my mother and daughter both say, "taken" at the same time, eyes never leaving the board.

"Share the table, Littlebiggle," I say.

"There's nowhere left to sit," my mother says.

The older woman has already moved off, unphased by the rejection. She perches at the end of a plastic couch, breaking leaves off the fica and nibbling on them.

My mother triple jumps my daughter's black discs. "So Argemina, what are you getting up to these days?"

They both make the non-verbal tics of conversation. Grunts of assent. Head nods. Hmmph's and how interesting's.

Later, when my daughter is in the nurse's station learning how to sort pills, I hold my mom's hands. From the outside, you would never know she was mindsick. But every once in a while, she turns her head and says things like "I know. I KNOW!" so softly.

"Mom," I say, "please don't encourage this pretend friend thing."

"What pretend friend?"

"Mom. Argemina."

My mother holds my gaze for a long time. Perhaps it is really a few seconds. Perhaps it only feels like eons because I never look in her eyes anymore—they are either blank from meds or frenetic with all the things she wants to say but won't, knowing what I'll have to do next.

"Just because you can't see someone doesn't mean they aren't real."

I sigh.

I cringe under her expression, resenting it too. Pity. Her poor befuddled daughter. This person who is bound by the laws of physics and reality which she discarded decades ago. I am stifled. I am repressed. I am the grandchild of people who met in an insane asylum. I am the mother who watches and waits, for myself, for my daughter.

At home, my daughter is back in the yard, this time with bubbles. She blows slowly, making large, gamboling orbs. She blows quickly and they are small and whisperfast.

"That one!" she yells, laughing as they pop. "That one, Argemina! That one!"

And they rise and swirl in the air and eventually pop Pop POP!

cul•ti•vate
v. to prepare the soil for the growing of something new

She is late cultivating her garden this year. Every year. Always the same routine: she sees the neighbors two houses up in their gloves and hats, kneeling on their foam mats with little rakes and trowels in their hands. It's time. Her own plot—a long, wide stretch beside her driveway—is covered with tiny weeds. Clover. Sheep's sorrel. Ragwort. Slender Speedwell. It is almost too bad they must go.

But go they must. She brings out her garden claw and starts at the corner closest to the garage. Strike, twist left, twist right, lift, move. Progress in six-inch increments. A quarter of the way down, she begins to feel little white blisters germinating on her palms. Tiny at this stage, by day's end, they will be the size of oyster crackers and nearly as thick. Why she doesn't take ten seconds to put on her gloves first, she never knows.

Never knowing what she might find when she begins this yearly cultivation makes for a kind of low-rent, occasionally macabre treasure hunt. When they first moved in and pulled up the overgrown nest the previous owners called a yard, they found marbles enough to fill a jar. And a condom wrapper. Both, she suspects, left by their son, at different stages. It was almost sad to place the sea of sod down upon that treasure trove. What else might we find, she asked her husband, turning over spade after spade just to see. Junk, he had said, more junk. Still, he let her dig around while he hauled the sod up from the pallet at the curb, and she found a bone. Probably a cow bone, possibly deer, but it had chilled her to hold it in her hands, hard and ivory under its layer of dirt. She stopped digging then, worried it might have been human.

Human bones are weak, porous. Her husband's turned out to be utterly permeable. By the time they found it—the doctors themselves a particular kind of gardener—it had spread from his spine into his femurs, then his arms. They dug into him, opened him up with their scalpels like the handweeder she uses to probe the earth. They eased out as much as they could find, replanted marrow and plasma, drew his skin back together like she might delicately mulch around the strawberries in spring.

By the next spring, he was gone. It was the only year she beat her neighbors to the task. Morning to night, she was out there, digging and digging and digging. Clumps of mud and compost clung to her clothes, her shoes, her hair, hitchhikers into the house, into her bed, kneaded into balls in the fretting tumble that was her sleep, as though she was remaking a mudman husband. The neighbors brought her easy-to-freeze casseroles. They offered to do the weeding for her, but she couldn't bear the thought of someone else's hands in her soil.

The soil gives way beneath her claw, just as she lets out a yelp of pain and sees the white skin of the blister, soft like a baby's ear, so pale, it is nearly transparent, tear away from her palm and a bubble of clear liquid rises. The claw has sunk halfway into the ground. She pulls it out and looks down into the maw of dirt, the sides of the opening holding together as little pink wormtails wriggle and slide back into sweet, cool darkness.

The darkness scares her, but still she forces herself to reach down into it, to grab a handful of dirt and bring it up into the light. It could have been a rathole, her husband's voice says to her, himself always the wary one when it came to animals of the night. He was terrified of possums, had once been chased by a raccoon in a gathering twilight on one of their last walks round the neighborhood. But when she removes her hand, it's clutching a fistful of tiny toy soldiers. Plastic and green. Holding rifles and walkie-talkies, some lying on their bellies with binoculars to their eyes. Handful after handful, she brings up the bodies of these soldiers. By the end, she must lay on her stomach, arm extended until she's groped for them all.

All of the soldiers line up on her driveway. She brings over the hose and sprays them as gently as a mother might wash a baby in the sink. They still fall over, small as they are, so she fills a bucket of water and dips them in one by one, running her fingers over the ridges of their plastic, using a fingernail to dig out from under chins and in the small cracks between bodies and arms, legs and the plastic platform upon which they stand. The soldier with the bayonet stabs into her opened blister and she drops him in the bucket, clutching her palm with her other hand as a little pindrop of blood rises to the surface of that delicate, vulnerable skin. She thinks about kicking over the bucket, stomping on the soldier, tossing him back into the hole.

The hole is lit through with the sun shining at just the right angle, and this is when she sees it, there at the bottom. One last time, she reaches down, finds the little plastic baggy shimmering in the slim rays. There is a note inside. She opens the bag. His handwriting triggers the synapses of her brain before the words take shape.

"You're doing great. Keep up the good work." On the other side, tiny in a corner: #3 of 8.

She grabs the cultivator and jams it into the earth again. Both hands are blistered and bleeding. Her stomach demands sustenance, but still she digs. She digs and she digs and she digs. She will find each piece of him in that rich, black earth. And once done, she will finally be ready to plant.

Laqueum quia Claire

The Tower of London lays in the heart of the city, a square stone citadel that once touched the waters of the Thames, dominating the skyline when London was a village of low, thatch-roofed buildings, its inhabits bent-backed and low themselves, toiling, toiling, pulling life from its muddy banks, pouring death in too. Now, it is a white and tan speck amongst great grey behemoths with names like the Gerkin, the Shard. You'd think this castle was the precursor to the city. First, the Tower, then a village seeking shelter, chicks to a mother hen. But first it was the village. Down into the loam of primal people, this village. Always people first. Then rulers. William and his metal-helmeted men streaming from a longship, proclaiming victory, progress, protection that begins with pen and book, inventory and taxes. If the Tower could speak, it would be William's voice coming from the ancient mortar. "Listen up, you lot."

"Listen up, you lot," the Yeoman Warder shouted. "We're now standing before St. Thomas' Tower, what was once the home of Edward I and his family. Inside, you can tour his throne room and bedchambers, even see his chamber of the stool." Claire turned to follow where he gestured, keeping watch for Adam's bobbing head, a finger at the bridge of his glasses, his shuffling gate that proxied as a run. So often of late, she'd catch him from the side of her eye and she'd almost call him by another man's name, becoming that little girl crying out for the hunched paternal back heaving the last box into their wood-paneled station wagon.

She tapped her mother's shoulder. "Let's go in." Her mother glanced back at the tour, then the direction Adam had gone. She shrugged and followed Claire.

Holding the wrought-iron chains, the two women climbed the stairs toward Edward's keep. The tour group moved off, following the black hat of the beefeater. They were heading toward the chapel to view, amongst other things, the graves of wives with misplaced heads. Claire identified with that feeling, her entirety contained in a soaring head, flying away from everything else below. What does innocence matter when you are in your shift and a hooded man is arranging your body to serve his purpose?

Her mother was panting by the time they entered the castle.

"Will Adam know where we've gone?"

Claire shrugged, but when her mother's eyes narrowed, she went on in the too-bright manner she'd adopted whenever she spoke about Adam or her marriage. "He's resourceful. Besides it's a square stone box. Where could we hide?"

But they could hide anywhere, so long as they kept moving. They could keep one another in constant orbit, rotating from one display to the next. And movement wasn't always necessary. Wasn't she hiding when she lay still in Adam's arms, when she smiled instead of screamed? The women whose bones lie tangled under the chapel floor—those women knew how to hide right where everyone could see them. Or maybe the problem was they didn't.

"If you say so." Her mother moved off, reading the placard above a display with her hands cupped behind her back.

Claire sat in the small bayed window in the throne room. She watched other tourists drift across to the model castle under a large glass box, where her mother was also now standing. A video streamed on the opposite wall, but Claire never caught it beginning to end.

She was glad for this moment alone. It had been a gamble to invite her mother to break away with her, but Claire couldn't risk losing her, simultaneously fearing what this privacy opened the door to. She was like a hungry blind mole, chasing the fetid fruit of her daughter's possibly rancid marriage. She lacked tact and timing. Just the other night, she'd cornered Claire with more wheedling questions, even though Adam sat on the other side of the flimsy walls in their vacation flat watching some British sit com.

Shifting her weight, Claire felt something beneath her. Fingers grazing the coarse grain of old stone, she found it, slippery as silk. A locket. Inside, one half showed an image of Anne Boleyn and on the other, her daughter. On the front, the letters of Anne and Elizabeth's names laced together. It must have been something purchased in one of the Tower's many gift shops and dropped here or fallen.

How many years ago had she lost it, that necklace, so very like this one in her palm? Back then, her mother's eyes had darted to the window, possibly looking for the sparkle of opal in the grass, perhaps under the tree. It had been a gift from Claire's father, an anniversary present Claire often pleaded to wear. Finally, one warm day in September, her mother relented with a caution to be careful, be ever so careful, as she placed it around Claire's neck. Years later, she would wonder if losing it had been the cause of it all. If perhaps all any woman could do was to be careful, be ever so careful.

But that day, her mother started the vacuum, something she did when she needed the rush of air to silence the gale within. Claire returned to her search for the necklace until night drew long and close around her, and she watched from the branches of the crabapple tree as her mother wept into the sink. Tomorrow she would search again, but she woke to the grumble of her father's mower.

Someone would come searching for the necklace, it was one of the nicer items the gift shop sold, not something one walks away from. She ought to leave it where she found it, there in the speckled light from rippling panes of old glass. Instead, she dropped it into her purse. She followed the arrows on the wall marking where she was to go next.

How We Do Things around Here

They were a youngish couple, childless, industrious. This is about all we could piece together from what we had that first week: a man and woman heaving rolls of sod from the pallet at the curb to their yard, the For Sale sign plucked from the parking strip and lying cattywhompus across the sidewalk. By sunset, they had an emerald sea stretching down the short hill of their front lawn and the man toasted everyone who passed with an upraised beer, the other hand ready to shoo eager dogs away. You'd have thought they were like us.

Attempts at conversation wilted, they fell over flat like the stalks of foxglove the man weed-whacked to a pulp one early Saturday morning.

We only ever learned what they did for work. He, a doctor, a type of specialist none of us had ever heard of, one of but two in the whole city, which accounted for his long and erratic hours, how he'd drag the trash down to the curb at 4 am on Monday mornings, waking those who lived to each side with the stuttering of his wheel-less bins.

She was a freelancer of some type which we had also never heard of and which some of us suspected might be the most modern adaptation of the stay-home wife. She left the trash bins at the curb half-way into the week. Once, we thought to be neighborly and drug it all the way back up their driveway. But there she was, watching us, glaring we assumed, through the large window while her arms flailed. But it was some strange calisthenic routine she followed from the screen of her computer. After that, we left them down there until he could be bothered with it, again at some god-awful hour of the morning, and we just shook our heads as we veered around them on our ways to work.

He left early, came home late, might wave if one of us happened to be out. For many months, we began to sight her like the elusive Cooper's hawk that sometimes landed in our trees, fleeting, wings still extended, taking off again by the time you could call anyone else to come corroborate what you'd seen. But toward the end of May, she was suddenly always on the porch, avoiding eye-contact and knitting. The ball of yarn often rolled down the steps into the detritus of leaves and dust and anthills forming at the base of the front stoop. But she didn't seem to mind reeling in yarn flecked with twigs and moth wings and other things. Just wove it all in.

We tried to ask questions. Be neighborly. How were they settling in? What was she making? But we were met with terse answers. Fine. Oh nothing. The most anyone ever got was "it's about the process. Not the product" and we weren't sure if she was talking about marriage or knitting. We accepted they were waving neighbors like the old Japanese fellow down the street, nice as can be, for whom waving was the only option because no one could understand him.

Finally, the thing was undeniably a blanket. Not square shaped. Rather odd-looking really. But so large! What else could it have been? We thought she might be getting a little bigger, a little rounder about the middle, but sitting down, it was hard to tell.

And then they were gone for many days. We watched their house for them because that's the kind of street we are. We poked their mail all the way through the slot until it fell with a heavy thud on the stack of mail on the other side. We looked for packages so we could bring them in to our own homes and keep them safe.

Then a light came on behind the curtains. And the next day, the woman was back on the porch, very pale. The blanket on her lap. The needles gone. She pulled the yarn out row by row, the crinked coils gathering at her feet. That night she went inside and left the pile there, where it stayed for many weeks until the two moving vans arrived and movers put the boxes with her name in one truck and his name in the other.

Within a week, a Sold sign sat at a jaunty angle across the realtor's name. This is a good neighborhood. It was never going to take long. A lesbian couple moved in. Friendly. Returned our plates with similar gestures of neighborly goodwill. Cookies sometimes. Or banana bread. They knew how this works.

They swept the pile of yarn into a black bag and set it in the bin, already at the curb by Sunday evening.

Check one, check check

Tabitha sat up from where she'd been lying on the couch, arms crossed, brows so furrowed, they might've tied themselves in a bow, yelling before I even had my coat off.

"What the hell, Dad! You spy on me?"

"Hey, we don't say hell in this household. And what are you talking about?" But I already knew. She was planning to use the teacher in-service day to clean that mess-scape she crawls out of, and while I applauded her initiative, I spent the day in an anxious sweat hoping she wouldn't find my shame. But there it was on the coffee table: her baby monitor, covered in nine years' worth of dust, discovered under her bed where I'd hidden it a few months after the funeral.

Tabitha ran upstairs. Down came the receiving end, pillaged from the back of a drawer in my own room after what must have been a long episode of rummaging.

This was no time for pots or kettles.

The next morning, I wiped down the monitor and receiver. Clean things are always easier to deal with.

When I tried to offer Tabby extra Cheesier-than-cheese eggs, she stuffed her books into her backpack, tramped out the sliding door, and kicked an apple fallen from the tree by our back deck, the one Janet planted when the test turned pink.

The tree had only lived seven seasons when Janet died. The night after we buried her, I went to Tabby's room and tried to tell her the story Janet made up for her, a tale about a unicorn named Sparkleheart and a rabbit, Glitterears. But Tabby put a hand on my arm and said, "nevermind, Daddy," by which she meant I wasn't doing it right.

That phrase became a harbinger when the ghost of my wife walked behind her eyes.

So I put the monitor under her bed and would turn it on when she started spending too much time in her room alone. Mostly, she was crying. At first, I went to her, and she let me hold her and I would be grateful that her gulping sobs swallowed my own. Then she started to yell at me if I entered without knocking first. But if I knocked, she told me to go away. Sometimes, she didn't even acknowledge I was there at all.

It was all I had, that monitor. So I would sit on the end of my bed, hunkered around that slim connection, watching the screen light up from yellow to red until the lights went silent and all that came through were the soft rumblings of my daughter finally at rest.

"What say we watch *Dirty Dancing*, huh?" I held the DVD aloft as soon as she came in.

"That show's for babies."

I took a gander at the image of Patrick Swayzee, topless and beefy, holding a leotard-clad Jennifer Grey aloft in a lake. "This is decidedly not for babies."

"Well, it's gross to watch a movie like that with your dad." And back upstairs she went.

I couldn't argue with that logic, but it had once been our thing, watching this movie, a bowl of popcorn between us, sliced apples on the coffee table.

Until she started talking on the phone.

By 12, weeping alone transitioned to chatting. At first, her calls to friends were banal, innocent: coordinating scrunchie or shoelace colors, which Barbies to bring to the sleepover. I was happy. At first. To hear her connecting with friends. Engaging. Giggling. Being a child in ways a dead parent too often takes with them.

But over time, that innocence faded into neurotic discussions about school politics, what other girls, older girls, were wearing, whether using tampons means you're destined to be a slut. Worst of all was the way she talked about her friends, revealing to Brittany what Stephanie had told her in confidence, the next night, laying Brittany's secrets bare on the altar of teen-girl brutality, the blade still crusted from the slaughter of Steph's angsts. Never once did I hear her reveal anything of import about herself, only weak-tea intimacies I was fairly certain were lies anyway.

I listened and fumed. Perhaps this was the punishment I deserved—to hear the person I loved most in the world become a nasty little shit.

Tossing the DVD case on the coffee table, the two little soldiers of my secret agent army before me, I heard Janet calling from the nook where she used to read and watch birds and knit. About apples not falling far from trees.

The next morning, Tabby stayed for breakfast but refused to speak.

"Tabbybear, listen." I scooped an extra helping of eggs onto her plate. "I just forgot that thing was under there."

"No. You didn't." The tilt of the head, the way her eyebrows scrunched together, the thin line of her pursed lips. She wasn't letting me get away with anything, just like her mother.

I reached for the monitor and receiver, one in each hand. "No," I said. "I didn't." I expected her to storm off, let this fall and pick it up another day, but the only move she made was to snap open her napkin, smooth it across her lap, and fold her hands over her plate. Waiting.

So I told her everything. About how I needed her, how she needed me, how grief makes you do stupid things like tell your dad to go away when you don't mean it, like spy on your daughter so you know she's ok.

She ate her eggs, and after, we started clearing bad apples from the yard. She would be late to school and I to work but we didn't care. We gathered them in our hands, some yellow, some red, bruised and rotten, smelling of sweet fecund death, and I told her how rotten fruit is food, nutrition. How nature intends them to fall and decay so the seed within can thrive.

We gathered some good ones too, and Tabby asked whether I thought they might be good in a pie. Or, maybe, sliced.

a pair of red curtains

Every village has that girl. The one other girls exclude and whisper about, spitting *puta* as she passes, unless the priest is nearby, and then they just spit. The one boys invite to walk along the deserted stretches of river, drawing her down with unnecessarily sweet words to lay in the dusty riverbank, under the shade of the *aragueney*, a drifting into their arms that she craves as much as they and thus, seeing their lust a mirror of her own, refuses to feel shamed for. It is an exchange without commitment. After, she rises, dusts off her skirts, and determines whether he is worth bringing here again. Most are not.

Over time, she watched each of these boys pair off with the whispering girls, avoiding her gaze when they passed in the street years later, arms that once enfolded her now laden with the mundanities of life: baskets from the market, a bag of seeds for the field, children from a bed growing colder each year.

Where is your *inhibicion*, her mother demanded. Your *verguenza*. You think you can do with your body as you please? And once, from her own mother's lips: *puta*. But what is inhibition and shame but worthless words? Words don't buy dresses or books or trips to the capital to attend the theatre. The only thing inhibiting her was money. That she couldn't do with as she pleased for she didn't have any of it. And in her village, there were but two means of acquiring it. The path of those who now walked with the boys of her youth held no appeal for her, and since marriage didn't seem much different than whoring—except you only got the one man and all those chores and children—she chose a life of no chores and all the men.

She left her mother's house at dawn on a holy day as a kindness. When her mother awoke and found the space beside her empty and cold, her daughter's meager belongings gone from her shelf, she would know and as she was heading to town anyway, she could throw in a prayer for this lost child and limp home. How little the daughter knew of the love that welled inside her mother, mistaking those constant trips to the *iglesia* as reflections of piety or belief, never realizing it was love for this daughter, love like a torrent, the constant incinerating heat of a lava flow, which sent the mother to church almost daily, not love for God.

She closed the lid on that part of her life and moved into an empty room on the ground floor of the town's only *posada*. The door of her bedroom opened into a storeroom that smelled sharply of beer and wine stacked in casks, and the other, to an alley and a canal off the river. She hung red curtains behind the one window of her single-room dwelling and made a candleshade out of red crepe paper which she set in the deep alcove of the windowsill and lit at night, her single advertisement. She smoked in a chair outside her open door with her skirts pulled up to her knees and worked the finger-lace knitting she had learned from Abuela Maria.

Her first customer was the inn's proprietor, a friend of her father's when he had lived, a man whose children she had suffered catechism classes with. Soon, other men from the village waited in the dusty alley outside her door, leaving her time to knit only very late and very early, bookending her days.

When she was not sleeping, she read. Fiction to philosophy. Poetry to history. Books lined the windowsill and floor, circling the small walls of her room, growing her horizons with each addition.

Word spread. Men from beyond the village and surrounding haciendas appeared at her door, milling along the riverbank so as not to rush their comrades.

In less years than she'd imagined, she was wealthy enough to purchase the inn from the owner and his wife, both old and hunched. The spring after this purchase, her mother died and she attended the funeral, pinning her chin to the clouds and never letting her aunts and cousins see how she crumpled under their withering glares, how she wanted to fling herself atop the casket and beg, beg, beg for the solace of forgiveness.

She hung the sets of lace curtains she had knit over so many years in the guestroom windows and took down the red ones for good, packing them away behind a barrel of beer. She bought new dresses that fell below her knees and exchanged her high-heeled red shoes for plain black flats better suited to long hours in the kitchen where she cooked the dishes of her *infancia: arepas, tequenos,* and of course *pabellon criollo*, to which she added European flare from books she ordered from the capital.

And she waited. She was courteous to the single visiting men, showed them her cooking was good, her conversation educated. She invited them to join her in the parlor for tea in the evenings; she hoped they would invite her for a stroll along the gaslit streets. For she had grown tired of seeing her clients at the town square on Sundays and feast days, happy with their round wives and exuberant children. And it was not too late.

She lay black lace over her hair and entered the cathedral from the side door, sidling into a pew when only the caretaker was present, pushing his haggard broom over the flagstones. Her knees grew the callouses she had once despised on her mother, the stigmata of her ignorant homage to a dead god, a god from whom she now begged one small good thing.

But still men showed up at the alley door, only a storehouse once more, her narrow bed turned on its side against the wall. They pushed crumpled, oily bolivars into her hands as they sidled inside, sunblind in the empty darkness, deaf to a story she can't untell.

Measure twice, cut once

Day 2

The sweater lay on the floor, one sleeve flung into the dark space under the bed.

"This is insane." Lillian held a sewer's plastic measuring tape, the end curled and bouncing as if this were a dance party and not a funeral march. "Over a sweater?"

Jess grabbed stacks of clothes. As he placed them in his bag, the piles crumbled in on themselves. He stuffed them down into the corners, his aversion to wrinkles apparently less important than his scramble to get it done. "Come on, Lil. It's not the sweater. It's the process behind it, what it means."

She sank to the bed. That had been her motto about all her knitting projects: It's not about the product, but the process. But this was Jess, this was different. She'd painstakingly measured and re-checked. Long evenings of cooling tea and streaming shows, Jess long since gone to bed and she, knitting by the light of a lamp. "Would you be doing this if my hobby was baking? Would you be leaving if I could broil fish and make Italian merengues?"

At first he was confused; then something else bloomed on his face. "All this time," he said. "I thought that sweater was for me."

"You're leaving for the wrong reason!"

"I was before." The front door opened, then closed. The neighbor's TV erupted in canned laughter.

Lillian drug the sweater out. She wept into the sleeve. Blew her nose on the elbow cabling.

Day 1

What a scramble to get it done. Jess would be home by quarter after, they were off to Lisa and Kyle's at six, the same Lisa who'd read some nonsense in a magazine about relationships and knit sweaters and curses. Lillian finished the last row of the 2x2 hem just as she heard his key in the lock.

"I finished!" She sidled up to him in the foyer, the sweater dancing in her hands, sleeves flapping, torso undulating.

"Ahh." Jess dropped his backpack on the table, hung his coat over the chair. "There it is. You really finished it." He hadn't been thrilled by the yarn, but once he had it on, he would like it, she was sure.

Lillian followed him down the hall, holding it up to his back. "I can't wait to see the look on Lisa's face. She's spent weeks on this meal? Try committing to knitting." She passed the sweater to him and closed the bedroom door, hopping foot to foot on the cold parquet. She heard the neighbor come home, the heavy slam of his front door, the almost immediate murmurs of his TV as if he were late for his real job. "Well?"

One look at Jess in the doorway. Too small, too tight. It clung to his neck, choking him. The sleeves ended well above his wrists. His belly showed, dark navel hairs curling around the 2x2 ribbing.

"Impossible!" She tugged at it. "But I measured!" She yelled into his face, right into his open mouth. "Every day!"

"I remember." He pulled it off, snapping threads. He let it fall to the floor on her side of the bed.

At dinner, he was cheerier than a person ought to be who had watched his beloved measure and make a thing just for him only to find it no longer fit. And that's what it must have been, Lillian concluded, as she chewed her carmelized carrots in their bourbon reduction. He had grown.

After dinner, Kyle and Jess took to the kitchen while Lisa led Lillian to the balcony, showing off the secluded jungle ambiance she had created with potted tropical plants and cross-hatched teak flooring from IKEA. Lisa refilled their sangria from a festive summer pitcher and reached into the foliage to click a series of buttons, after which the sounds of rasping crickets and a bubbling brook emanated from a pair of speakers hidden above. She liked to sing out the amount of money she had spent on these little beautifying projects, and it was, in fact, impressive that such a transformation had occurred on so slim a budget.

Lillian slurped from her glass. Why couldn't she just be satisfied with these kinds of domestic arts? Lisa was a kind of genius with food and decorating, turning whatever space she occupied into an ensemble, a theme. She cooked with ingredients Lillian had never heard of, with the flesh of animals that sounded like they ought to be on endangered species lists. They were transient things, disposable things. Even now, Lillian could hear one of the men scraping the remnants of Lisa's efforts into the garbage disposal, making a mush for sewer pipes that couldn't give two shits whether they received Kraft mac-n-cheese or pan-seared Greek swordfish with olive-pistachio sauce.

There was simply no comparison between what Lillian created and Lisa decorated. A completed sweater was only that, something done and put in a drawer, alongside its cousins that could have been—had been—bought online or picked up at any department store.

"So," Lisa said, easing into another matching teak chair. "The sweater."

Lillian groaned and for added emphasis, drained her glass and held it out for more. "It's fine." Though of course it wasn't. What had possessed her to send that text crowing that Lisa would finally see it finished before Jess even tried it on? "It was a bit tight."

Through the sliding glass door, they saw Kyle and Jess in the kitchen. Jess was tapping his forearms; then his hands went round his neck. Kyle patted his shoulder and shook his head. His laughter turned earnest, his head tilted, and he spoke, both men nodding and ending with a handshake before beginning to move toward them.

"It's fine." Lillian leaned over the balcony rail, watching a couple emerge from the ice cream shop that occupied the street-level space. "I'll restart it tomorrow. Measure him again, first thing he comes home."

Funeral Pyre

We found the pregnancy test behind the bathroom cabinet during the remodel. Perhaps I shoved it to the back of a drawer. Perhaps it later fell out into a dusty, black corner behind the towels and cleaning sprays. Perhaps when we ripped out the cabinet and the cheap composite wood shattered, it popped out into the rubble of plaster and dust balls. You never know how the bad penny gets where it is.

Problem was, this pregnancy test was supposed to have been burned five years ago. It was the last pregnancy test we ever hunched over, used three days after my thirty-eighth birthday and six years after we'd started trying. My husband pulled off his face mask, hands dusty from the demo, picked it up and held it out to me. On his face the same hurt and broken look. From his mouth, nearly the same hurt and broken words, "it's this one?"

Five years ago, he had asked, "this is the one?" and I had answered "yes," the lie rolling from my tongue easily, the snake of it hissing from my lips, curling into the empty space between us. It is a slippery word—"yes"—a word that slithers in the space between truth and not, living under the tip of our tongues, in that moist dark space where there simply is not enough room for all the truths too hard to swallow.

Five years ago, he threw the final betrayer into our little fire pit despite the July heatwave, and we held each other as our bodies grew moist with sweat. We watched the pink plastic boil and pop until the metal basin held nothing but ash. He has always been a man given to vast symbolic gestures, someone who performs his emotions with archaic rituals that push deep into the darkness of our primitive consciousness. The day we met, he was sitting on his stoop eating a bowl of soup sprinkled with the ashes of his grandfather, dipping bread he'd seasoned with tears he had cried and then churned into butter. Watching him, I prayed to whatever gods might be listening that I might be granted this tender man, rendered the custody of his delicate soul. It was hubris all along.

So when he told me what he wanted to do with it and I couldn't find the damn thing anywhere, I panicked. There was such purpose to his plan, such weight to his words as he snapped twigs and lined the fire pit with them. What else could I do? I peed on another one, and didn't bother to watch it.

Now, he threw it back on the rubble, walked down the hall, and out the front door.

We'd gone on a vacation after the event with the fire pit, two weeks in the Greek isles, catching rides with fishermen from one little harbor to the next, finding tucked-away hotels manned by sleepy, startled desk clerks, the language barrier no hindrance to our needs—praying hands tucked under our cheeks and our eyes closed, fingers dipping into imaginary bowls and coming to our lips. We swam into some caves at Kefalonia and clung to each other as we tread water, our knees bumping and bruising, turning the colors of the fetal fruits growing in the groves on the hillsides. Our tears replenished the waters of our dear child, we the parents of these tender teeming harbors. We made love like mad people, finally released from the calendars and the pills and the shots and the diets. We drank a bottle of wine at dinner almost every night. We bought every bit of touristy crap that caught our eyes and shipped it back home at exorbitant rates. We had years and years' worth of savings we wouldn't need for tuition or dance lessons or baseball-broken windows or emergency room visits. A kid on a beach at Ithaka sold us the last of his stale pot. We lay on a dock and smoked until the stars began to dance in the sky just for us. At the museum in Athens, my husband stared at an ancient amphora showing the funeral rites for a child: the laying out of the body, the procession, the cremation. He bought a replica of it in the gift shop and carried it swaddled in bubble wrap like a sleeping infant all the way home.

For the three days my husband was gone, I took washcloth baths in the basement mudsink. I stopped by the open bathroom door, the flood lamp still on, giving off a faint burning smell, and saw the test lying where my husband let it fall, the pink of it fainter with age and dust, except for the places where his fingers had touched. I wondered if I should call someone to finish it and though I looked up a number of bathroom remodelers, I couldn't bring myself to dial.

Then my husband was home again. He backed his car up the driveway and began unloading. The trunk was full of split logs, his clothes dirty and torn, shards of wood woven into his shirt, his neck covered in a fine woody powder. An axe with the price tag still dangling from its handle rode shotgun. We built a pyre in our backyard, laying the logs in a square frame, stacked atop one another. Up and up and up. Wordlessly, my husband entered the house, and when he came back, he held the entire bathroom cabinet in his arms, the test lost amongst all the other shattered splinters. And on top, the amphora, still protected by bubble wrap, dusty from its long, aching nap in the attic.

He placed it atop the pyre as gently as a father lays his child down for her final sleep. He struck a match and held it out to me.

Hook, Lift, Release

The boy focuses on the hook and the loom, the four rounds of red, followed by four rounds of yellow. Miranda, the nice one, comes over and nods at his work. Yesterday, she showed him how to blend the yellow and red yarns, making it look like one bleeds into the other, like a sunset. Like a fire. He sits at the table working on his loom hat while the other kids perform the planned activities.

On this day, his last, the counselors have brought in a TV and a laptop. A large green screen dangles from a tripod. The laptop's webcam picks up the image of whatever is in front of the screen, transmitting it in combination with another scene to the TV which is turned toward the rest of the campers. Until someone tells you what's happening on the TV, you don't know what the image is at all. This lack of knowledge is supposed to be fun.

The children shout what they see: a stream in a forest, a run-down house, a stairwell in an alley, a trampoline.

Deekan is having the first turn. Deekan is a first-turner kind of kid.

The counselors and other day-campers shout encouragement and ideas for what he might do. He pretends to cup water and lift it to his mouth, face curdling at the smell of it. He tiptoes past the run-down house, waving his hand in front of his nose like it farted. He lifts his knees high to climb up the stairwell, arms akimbo with exceptional sneakiness. Deekan jumps and jumps and jumps and jumps, and even from across the gym at his table with the hook and loom, the boy starts to believe it might be real. That somewhere someone is leaping toward the sun, hair lifting off their head like feathers.

But it isn't.

What is real is Deekan leaping about like someone having a fit or finding Jesus. Deekan in a yellow t-shirt bearing the camp logo—a beaver in a canoe—in the middle of a moldy-smelling gymnasium on a day his own mother would call hotter than a dog's balls. The beaver logo implies a sleep-away camp in a forest.

But it isn't.

What it is is a day-camp at an elementary school his case worker signed him up for while his mom is supposed to be—but isn't—in day treatment and meetings. The counselors bring in activities like this webcam and screen. The day before it had been a tennis-ball launcher aimed at the ceiling, each camper handed a racket and told to hit whatever they can until that whatever turned into each other. It is a distraction from what's waiting for them on the other side of the busride home: their houses, his own only slightly better than that one on the screen, containing mothers who are too tired from lumbering under the weight of inactivity, from struggling to curtail the wanting too much that comes from never having enough. Where fathers drink too much to forget all the not-knowing, not-having-done they've accomplished in the short span of their lives.

After snack—always apples and carrots, carrots and apples—they work on their loom hats together, using the hooks to catch the yarn and loop it over the pins one by one. He is farther along than anyone, and he works quickly, intent on finishing his hat today so he can take it home with him on the bus. Except home is not where he is going. He will get off at the wrong stop, telling the nosy bus-driver he's going to a friend's house. He'll follow the spire of Union Station downtown. He'll buy a Greyhound ticket for wherever is $42 away.

Evan, the mean one, blows his whistle signaling time to change activities. The boy continues to work—hook, lift, release; hook, lift, release—hoping Evan will forget he is there.

Miranda calls him over in a cheery voice. "Ok campers! Ok! Campers!" Evan pulls the loom out of his hands. Half the loops fall off, unravelling. Ruined.

"Now look what you did!" Evan says. It's almost the same tone his mother uses before it begins.

The boy tries not to cry as he sits against the wall and watches them rustle the parachute. Evan calls names, and the chosen ones crawl under the swishing slick fabric. He pulls his knees up tight. They lift the parachute high, catch a pocket of air, and pull it down under their bottoms. When the parachute descends, the whole weight of the sky coming down on them, he is rocking forward and back, trying not to remember the first day they did this. How the staticky fabric fused to his eyes and nose. The way the other children stood like statues, fingers in their mouths, some clinging to Miranda, as he writhed and screamed on the floor, begging it to stop. He's never had to do anything he didn't want to since that day, but still he has to sit and watch the activity as the meagerest form of participation. They glance to make sure he's there, then look away.

At the end of the day, he lobs a ball in the direction of the craft bins. He apologizes, then chases after it. He tucks a loom, hook, and yarn in his backpack. It's not his, but that doesn't matter. It will be nice to have something to work on wherever it is he's going.

Cotton Trail Queen

The body was lying at the bottom of the canyon. It gleamed white against the brown and ochre rocks. Well, except for all the bits that were red.

And there were a lot of red bits.

Haverly wakes to the sound of bleating. Very far away bleating. She shuffles out of her sleeping bag, stiffening when Jasper turns on his side. He has never been a morning person. Waking him to say something was bleating would earn her the look. Waking him to say she was going out to rescue a lost sheep would keep him pinned to her side, petulant as a child. Jasper had once described the military testing that had gone on—might still be going on—in these canyons since the 40s. All kinds of weird shit they're testing for, he'd said. She made sure he didn't mean radioactive, and he laughed. Further south maybe, he said, pointing west though Haverly didn't correct him. Would I take you somewhere like that? He held a hand gently against her navel and said, not good for a positive outcome.

And this camping trip was all about positive outcomes.

She holds yesterday's underwear over the zipper to quiet its purr.

Still, that bleating. Very far away.

She once believed every desert trail hid a secret oasis, a sparkling meadow of lush grass and wildflowers, lupines covered in bees, whippoorwills whipporing, and a stream running through. No meadow is perfect without a stream.

More than once, she has hiked miles beyond her intended trek, convinced that just over the next rise, just past the next arroyo, just beyond the dried-up streambed with its deep spider-webby cracks— just over *there*, she would find the meadow.

And maybe, wild sheep grazing, their lambs doing stiff-legged hoppy-dances.

She can imagine whispering these stories into the spiraling auricula of a very small ear, rubbing the soft lobe between thumb and finger as little eyes close, breath slow and even.

Haverly tips over each of her boots, tapping the soles, eyes averted, hoping she doesn't hear the plump thud of a snake falling out.

It happened to a friend of theirs. She pulls them on and heads down the hill.

The bleating grows closer. The shade from the mountain will begin its creep back to the base as the sun drags itself across a sky she cannot determine the color of. She has an hour before the baking sun reaches the tent and wakes Jasper. An hour before he begins packing up and they hike back to the trailhead and their car, an Impreza that has more than once refused to start on their return from a backcountry trip.

In 14 days, she will know. She says, positive outcomes, positive outcomes, over and over like a mantra.

Overhead, a low thundering grumble tells her a plane is passing but she cannot see it. The bleating. It seems to be coming from across the valley. The sound is not so much of a lost sheep, but a terrified one. A bleat that has turned into a scream.

What if it's gotten away from the herd and is now perched on some gnarly precipice overlooking the mystical meadow? She can see her friends happily crunching away on the pristine grass below, and she's cragfast above? Haverly's steps quicken, matching the rhythm of her heart. Perhaps she is going too fast, jarring things, shaking them loose, but then she reminds herself walking is good for blood flow, especially down there.

Cresting the next rise, she is certain it must be just over the next one. This must be it. She can almost smell the water. The queen anne's lace. And then there is a thud, like a garbage bag of vegetable soup hitting pavement. As she pulls herself over the last stand of rocks, she sees it down there.

The body of a sheep. It's almost completely unidentifiable as sheep. Flattened, torn. But there is the white fluff of its wool.

White where it isn't red, the body on the rocks an accusation like the stains on her underwear each month.

And it is no meadow down there. Just more desert canyon. A swath of dried-out landscape in more hues of tan than should be permissible.

Haverly lays down on her stomach, absorbing warmth from the rocks like a lizard. Her breath is fast and heavy, and she tries to feel for it as her belly heaves against the rock, a little pea somewhere in there.

There's the grumble of a plane again. Rolling over and shielding her eyes, she tracks the sound across the sky.

A giant B-52 with the cargo door open seems to float a million yearnings above. And then a fluff of white silhouetted against the black maw of the open cargo bay, and then that white is out into the sky. A perfectly formed oval cloud. Bleating as it descends.

She watches three more fall at regular intervals before the plane is out of sight. And she rises, warm and numb, leaden-footed and dry-eyed.

Back at the campsite, Jasper is sitting on one of the rocks they used for chairs last night. He rises and puts on his backpack, picks hers up and holds the straps at the ready.

He puts a hand to her abdomen and gives her a smile. Two weeks, he says, and waves his hands, fingers crossed.

And she throws herself forward in time, falling into that future where red on white might be the thing that kills her. Saves her.

We See She

The light slants across the window, pale and luminous from the gauzy curtain pulled across. She thinks it is some kind of visual barrier. She must. The way she dances, walks through the house in her bra after a shower, stands at the window picking her teeth. Sometimes her nose. Surely she must think no one can see her. But by night, with the light coming from within, those curtains are as transparent as windowpane.

We can see everything.

There is not much to see.

She eats bowls of ramen standing up, chopsticks laced in her fingers. Pizza too. Crumbs fall. She takes big long swallows of beer, guzzling it as she stands in the middle of the room and watches television. Sometimes she stands and reads. Stands and knits. Does she not have a couch? Does she have some political stance on the very *idea* of couches, or sitting?

It is not easy, this standing all day. So we can watch her.

Sometimes she goes through the salutation to the sun four times, maybe six. She spends entire days in her yoga pants.

The other rooms of her house have cedar shades tilted at a forbidding angle. We can only see in this one, the one directly across from ours. It is enough.

Now she is doing what looks like tai chi, her face turned toward the television in the corner.

What are you looking at? This from Paul, our roommate. It's his house actually, which we must acknowledge, makes us the roommates.

Sherry, we say. No, Charlene. Sh-something. She never closes her curtains.

It's a little creepy.

Yes, we say, doesn't she know everyone can see her?

We ask Paul if there are any more slices of pizza and when we remain standing before our window, making no indication we intend to get it for ourselves, he brings them to us, stacked on one plate, cheesey side to cheesey side, like pizza porn.

We chew and wonder if Sherry-Charlene has ever taken a yoga class or if all she knows is the sun salutation. If she's seen the coupon for the yoga studio on the corner. If she knows there is a tai chi group that meets in Laurelhurst Park on Sunday mornings. We've seen the ads in the *Portland Mercury* Paul leaves on the coffee table.

   She should really get out more, we say, brushing crumbs onto the floor.

   Doesn't she know there's a whole wide world out there?

Amy Foster Myer grew up in Indiana from sturdy German stock on her father's side and slightly flighty Irish stock on her mother's. An avid reader from an early age, she experienced the transformative nature of the written word, and is perhaps best known for being the child who required 20 minutes to choose which book to read on the way to the grocery store…a trip of 5 minutes.

Her inspirations have always been the strong women in her life: Her grandmother, who died on her 101st birthday and lived the hard, but blessed life of a farm wife: raising four boys, working the acreage that had been in the Myer family from 1836-2020, running a small business, and baking the best crescent rolls ever to cross your lips.

Her mother and three aunts: independent, boisterous, convivial women who regaled a rapt family audience with stories from their own childhood: pranks with duct tape and sisters hidden under beds and looking so similarly in high school, they could trick one another's dates into taking the wrong sister out.

And her high school English teacher who, in the great tradition of excellent English teachers everywhere, was unpopular with the slackerish students but uniformly appreciated by those who recognized her strict expectations and high academic standards as the foundation necessary for success. This teacher introduced her to Shirley Jackson and Jane Austen and without whom, Amy very likely wouldn't be a writer today.

Amy earned her MFA from Queens University of Charlotte. She lives in Portland, Oregon, with her wife, Sarah, and two daughters, Jane and Evalyn. When not writing, Amy is reading or knitting or baking or playing an instrument (seriously though: how many does one need to teach one's self?) or attempting watercolor painting.